THE SHARK CAGE

LAURA SEYMOUR

CinnamonPress
INDEPENDENT INNOVATIVE INTERNATIONAL

Published by Cinnamon Press
Meirion House
Tanygrisiau
Blaenau Ffestiniog
Gwynedd, LL41 3SU
www.cinnamonpress.com
The right of Laura Seymour to be identified as author of this work has been asserted by her in accordance with the Copyright, Designs and Patent Act, 1988. Copyright © 2015 Laura Seymour. ISBN: 978-1-909077-75-1
British Library Cataloguing in Publication Data. A CIP record for this book can be obtained from the British Library.
Designed and typeset in Palatino by Cinnamon Press. Printed in Poland
Original cover design by Adam Craig.
Cinnamon Press is represented in the UK by Inpress Ltd www.inpressbooks.co.uk and in Wales by the Welsh Books Council www.cllc.org.uk

Acknowledgements

'The Last Dragon' was first published in *Envoi* and the Cinnamon Press anthology *Journey Planner* (2014).
'My Past Life 2: Professional Dowser, 1973', 'The National Grid' and 'X' were first published in *Orbis* 167 (2014)
'Mick' won third prize in the 2013 Alan Sillitoe Open Poetry Competition and was published on the Alan Sillitoe website.
'Heretics 'was first published in *Ambit* 218 (2014).
'The Shark Cage', 'Mick Dresses as a Zebra', and 'May Day' were first published in the anthology *May Day* by Cinnamon Press.
'Visitation', 'Carol', and 'My Leg' were first published in *Glitterwolf* Halloween Special Issue (2014).
'Cutting Chips' came third in the Ledbury Open Poetry Competition 2014 and was published on their website.
Thank you to all who read and commented on the manuscript: Helen Ivory, Katrina Naomi, Martin Figura, Sandy Steel, Ruth Mariner, and Stuart Bell, to Mercedes Rodríguez-Rubio, and to my family.

Contents

The Shark Cage

Carol

(Imagined) Homecomings

Maria

The Shark Cage

The Shark Cage

My father was pouring champagne into the sea,
last time I saw him. He and Mick who had eight
cars (my dad had seven) were laughing. You
dared one of them to climb into the shark cage.
You licked your lips, red as a court summons.
My dad strapped on a diving mask, kept on his suit,
festooned the cage with pale meat running cerise as beanflowers.
Some guests hung canapés on the bars with their earrings:
'we'd like you to meet the better class of shark'. Your
looks were free, your locks were yellow as gold. You
braced one stiletto on the yacht's rim, winched
him down. When you hauled the shark cage up again,
its middle bars were wrenched apart, and it was
                                                    empty.

My grandparents said it was a holiday:
I stayed at theirs during the investigation
(they found nor hair nor watchstrap of him).
They offered me anything. The room I liked best
contained their old toys. A rag doll, her china face
cracked dirtily like a net thrown over her head.
A poster of a man in the Luftwaffe, targets 1, 2, 3
on his head, heart, trigger hand. A diver
with a tube at his back: I dropped him
in my Coke, midnight water,
blew into the tube, and he ascended,
breaking the icecream float like heavenly clouds.

The National Grid

My grandmother conquers indigo fields in her gumboots:
smell of raw ragwort flourishing with disease;
smash of beeches; silence of badgers running like stop-
motion black and white films.

In the middle of the big meadow, she climbs a pylon,
hefting floral-socked ankles above neck
height. Her hair is a fistful of knitting needles;
her skirt is a scalene triangle outlined with yellow highlighter.

She pulls the plug on the National Grid.
In the darkness that follows, her milk-glass eyes
sweep the whole curved land from Paris to Argentina.

Next time, she tells herself, next time,
she'll see the tiny red night-light flicker
of my father's heart.

Chickenpox

The window cushions
fold their elbows.
When I knock at my chest,
growlers slide in teddies' throats:
I love you! Up the Empire!
seeps through plywood.

I jab a beaker into the curtains,
slide a postcard underneath.

Floating in the glass,
through its frog-skin of fog,
a kingpin's eyes sear
red spots
on all my arms.

Trainers hang on the telephone wires,
making the boys stop.

My skin stuns;
parched, veinless fingers
jounce my python-skin pram,
crack snakes for breakfast.

My grandmother works under cover of night
with camomile cream,
wincing at the sirens.

I set
firm into a pillar
strong enough
to hold up the new Kingpin Carpark.

His eyes itch,
sealed next to my skin.

Gryphaea

I want the rock that sloshes with water
from the poles of Mars.
Liquid that was charmed
to splitting needles like a startled hare,
that drummed furred feet on the sides
and now sleeps silky and leaden
and tangy with barbiturates.

Baskets of heavy spirals,
50p. Stopped clocks,
they seem on the brink of turning.

The prize exhibit, in a smear of slate,
'a £50' dog-tag around her neck,
is a mother. Her jaw a surprised thief's
discarded hacksaw, belly a motte
moating four tiny kit-replicas
of herself. Blanketless childbed.

The proprietor slops up on slouchy shoes.
He rattles a cardboard box of oysters,
dripping with stone, packed
into a Roman tortoise: pennants, cuirasses, guns.

I remember to press his toes
and feel nothing but air.

The Last Dragon

Two shoeboxes painted green
with sharp ice cream tub
teeth see-
saw, blinkers, over my
face. My stick-on eyes goggle.

I am the last dragon, pupils blackening
my candy loot with coronets of flame.
Asbestos curls from my nostrils
heat my lair
in the yapping basalts of Snowdonia,
blasting with blastoma anyone nearby.

My navel, caked over with pulsing scales,
is erased from time:
I have never been tied to another.

May Day

We wrap our gunpowder in cartoons;
mine depicts a rectangle of butter
with long-lashed eyes and weak yellow legs
leaping lustfully onto a clove-picketed ham.

We lose my grandfather immediately to Satan
(so we call the person in the garden whose gaze
clogged our lungs with the ashes of Judas,
Brutus, and other souls despairing for eternity).

We progress from a matchstick
to a clunky oxtail fuse,
from powder scraped from cap-guns
to saltpetre, nitre, magnesium for colour.

My devil's feet of plastic, air,
and synthetic brown fur cut my skin
so much I am glad when my own feet grow
shaggy, my toes fuse, nails curl.

I only realise our regimented planning
was all chaos when my skin dances off
to the forest, when the nurses roughly
pull drips from our arms.

Mick

My cloak muffling my mouth,
I tell his secretary
I want to borrow ten pounds
for sweets.

When I arrive Mick hastily hides
some papers in his desk and holds out a twenty.
I paw the carpet
with boar's spattering hooves,
gawping tusks, charge
and punch him.
His chest caves in, his plaster head
rolls off: 'lollipops, chocolate change,
fizzy rubber snakes, jelly blackberries', it says.

I score a ring in charcoal round him.
slash and stab his business suit.

The room fills with loose organs
of straw. There is not even
a lump of coal
for the heart that stoked my father's
to crime.

He staggers to his feet and puts his head on,
'Have twenty'.

Sheltered Housing

The estate agents carved their soles
into cows' hooves
when they carried my grandparents away.

I hand out leaflets with descriptions:
'Man. My face,
floating on his neck
like a printed erratum slip pasted
over a better word.'

'Woman. Every time she bites
an apple my mouth fills
with pixellated fruit'.
I did not pause
at the frantic half-moons in the mud.

In their new bungalow, my grandparents
watch lemon cake fur
and stiffen, a process
of evolution. They cough
gravel. Grit
seeps from their eyes.

When a city worker shoulders
them, trying to make them leave
the pavement,
their bodies are rooted
calcite.

Giro

The bank clerk has frank curls
childish and delicate as tansy,
so I ask him to help with my shoes.
He bends in an instant
and rights them.

The deep nails
sunk between my toe-bones
latching a roughened iron pipe
to each of my soles had pulled
left. Bruises bulge, purple crocuses
breaking snow with their foreheads.

The streets are glass
and I must not
slide.
Climbing up each day to pay in wages,
spending them all on the way down.

The day I skive work,
we poach nextdoor's Victoria plums.
You spin me, you who turned
and heard me.
My feet flex,
 whistling, supple as swans'
necks.

The Sieve Factory

I chose the worst job:
punching holes in sieves.
I won't be seduced
into enjoying something
I am just doing for money.
The metal stomachs whine
as I push my fingers in,
Doubting Thomas
a thousand times a day.

In the 'SIEVE TESTING ROOM', ladies cry,
whether because they killed their husbands,
or because noticing each new delivery
of sieves (and relinquishing
the last ones worn by water
to bent haloes, bird sterna)
is their way of keeping track of the centuries.
They have become
haughtily polite.

I fill my pockets with sharp metal circles,
planets heaped
in a burning catastrophe,
thread them
into a dress for my son.
He is the queen of the moonlight,
bumped by mice in wet grass,
oblivious of the roadside.

House Spider

He wasn't born like this,

*super-clever, super-adapted, super-**strong**!!*

How could she know he'd made a web
here. His eight legs jerk her
teacup
up and down to her
mouth, shut the door, turn
the clock hands
to past the last bus home.

He'd seemed so gentle,
so geeky. Only too late
he reveals his secret identity:

*super-clever, super-adapted, super-**strong**!!*
PUBLIC MENACE!

He crouches over some
thing frozen on the carpet. He is so pains-
taking, it is like an act
of love.

The cure for arachnophobia,
the lady at the zoo tells me later,
is to touch them.
I stroke his black hair at the nape
soothingly, goodbye.

Where Did You Get That Lipstick?

I must sail a boat for Greenpeace,
no time to change
out of my school uniform.
Stretching my arms
to the ship's notched wheel,
mitten strings cut
across my back.

You hover above me
in a spherical pink helicopter,
feathered all over and powered
by two lolloping ostrich plumes.
Your hair piled high over a cushion,
your fists smash factorycheap cakes.
Loveletters from notmyfather,
puff in French grey smoke
from your exhaust.

Whooping at the controls,
you are a tadpole smeared
behind the orange windscreen.
You fire and latch and drag
into a whale's shy back,
its courtyard fountain.

The sea is a cage of ferrets,
squirming, completely red
beneath you.

Carol

Carol

Carol has filled her study with specimens
of the previous bodies she inhabited.
A cuttlefish gropes piteously at me
with tentacles like ribbons on a straightjacket.
A lone baby's foot, lined with stars,
presses the thick glass jar. How I would cherish it.

I see at one time she was a piece of quartz
in the path I trod daily.
In another an unscratchable snake
swiping throbbing fangs
a metre from my neck
in a train station.

I really can't move on with Carol
until I've smashed those jars.
Their contents
lurch like fighting cats onto the carpet.
They weld together:
a long-separated family on Judgement Day,
pores getting wider and wider,
to feel and feel and feel.

Carol grinds a heel into the mess.

In the north, there is a crack
in the basalt,
where continents sail in opposite
directions.
It seems I stand
on the North American plate,
watching her on the European one.
Then she is beside me

       still hot from leaping.

Carol Steals Giraffes

Their shins make shifting
mango murals round the edges
of the tiny auditorium.

No one has used
this theatre since the 80s.
Out front, it is a dirty white blank
between 'Dan's Food' and a launderette.
Carol stole
the key beneath the pillow
of the manager, impoverished
and bedbound.

Carol pretended to some out-of-luck redecorators
she was from the National Trust
to have the tiered seating
rudely ripped out.
She penned the giraffes
behind the seating-rails.
I can't tell if she's put giraffe food
in the top boxes.

At a weathered garden table on the stage
we eat amid the breathing of giraffes:
vicious orange lobster bisque,
bluefin tuna, twitching blocks of caribou.
We finish with tea, milk from her own fridge
about to go off. I loll
in the pit, she spoons
smashed Viennese whirls into my mouth.

I suppose the giant giraffes
convince me of the grandness of our passion.
I hope she put them out to grass
after, try not to think of the key
slipped silently back under
the damp feather pillow,
the giraffes looking at each other,
locked in firmly, their voices not loud enough,
until the first one sags.

By Appointment Only

My cuffs lie wet
against my wrists.

I knelt on the way to tonight's meeting,
scrabbled in a puddle,
held up hands ringed with worms.

Any water compels me
to plunge my fingers in and seek
his fingers reaching up.
I always feel
his nails,
before they slip away.

At allotments, I inspect
every ranked rainwater-butt
studded with pendulous
snails. I've pushed through parents
in chinos and cocktail dresses
to rummage in the kids' paddling pool.

The lady beside me in tonight's circle of chairs
is a far worse case.
Her buckled swimhat and her dress
made of a marine freight sack,
'Special Delivery' in pale rose writing
along her back,
show that she is always ready to go.

When we make puppets,
hers is a purple octopus
tentacle with pink suckers
that cuddles round her waist,
stroking and waving gently
on a wire.

In the end, she kills herself
with tablets she'd been stockpiling for months,
pockets her makeup,
takes to the sea.

Tonight, we can choose any shell
from the jar. I pick after a cruise ship singer
and a farmer who runs a video camera
all night by his pool in Cumbria
a to see if the girl who crawled in one night-
tick-tock of her legs –
will ever crawl out.
We each hold
a crab, razor, whelk to our ears

and listen.

Child Support

Because he cannot keep his daughter,
he lines Coke
bottles, narrow drinking end
downwards, on the haha
wall. She claps as he runs along them,
feet skimming their upturned
bottoms
without knocking a single one over.
They turn the sun sticky, wasps
make them buzz like electric bulbs
on the red carpet to a premier.

X

aspires to reach the breadline one day,
painting her face matte white,
except her nostrils,
cucumber-tendril curves
outlined with kohl.

X charges me £20 an hour
because I agree to share my sessions
with a heavy man, his baggy three-piece suit
green as chickweed.
He claims Boudicea skewered him centuries ago,
and wants a chance to remonstrate with her.

X sees faces in her lamps.
She drinks unfermented grape juice,
eats black rusks, the flesh of poodles.

Her table is a clatter
of tomato sandwiches on cardboardy bread.
She uses them to ground herself
after helping her clients
to remember their past selves.

Boadicea Scents Hugo Boss

Boadicea pauses at a portly Roman soldier,
a bronze eagle tilting
his helmet groundwards,
his neck tender
with Hugo Boss aftershave.
She takes a breather
before dispatching this easy prey.

He gargles
'Hwaet, Hwaet',
sure that this means 'wait',
and holds out a photograph
of Boadicea's statue in London.

Boadicea's heart melts,
so rarely she receives presents!
Her scar-starred hand stretches
to caress her tonguetied enemy.

The sky torques,
knots.

The man is on his back;
he smells plastic, celluloid.

My Past Life 1: My Leg, 1907

My wife perches stoutly on a cow's skull,
milking. Her blue and white striped bag
traps trout in the river.
I see their wishing-teeth.
I promise her, today I'll be home for dinner.

I gatecrash a townhouse party that evening:
pipe salmon mousse into my mouth,
purloin gin fizz from the waiters.
Because I can sing the old songs
they let me stay.

On my sobering coastal walk, my troubles begin.
I've a vague idea of bringing her a shark,
wrestling it on our Tudor-rose-pink rug.
Instead, I drown.

Jellyfish, like poisoned wedding veils,
cling and kill. The airbags on the faces
of zooming gannets press my ribs.
A chocolatey flurry of eiderducks
grabs a taste of me too.

For six years, chin wobbling amid laughing
puffins, my wife looks for me, drops me
bit by bit into her blue-and white-bag.
She gives the full bag a Christian burial:
if a whole body's buried, the soul can rest.

After she dies, I spend a century
watching my leg float towards Greenland,
balanced like a yoke bearing
the two full pails of the Arctic and Atlantic.
It is the final part of me left unconsecrated:

I need it.

My Past Life 2: Professional Dowser, 1973

'I could always sense minerals where they slept',
I tell the man whose voice is greased
with quails' eggs, truffles, deer,
his suit the colour
of snipped-up dusk;
'I can feel metals, too.
I form an arrow with my hands
–knuckle, blood–
and they greet me like friends.
An effervescent handclasp
is diamonds fathoms down.
Gold presses its belly against mine.
I submit politely to tin's frank
but meaningless kiss on the brow'.

He's bought me dinner, wine
minerally as limestone
stencilled with creatures.
My old scars open.
Ancient thoughts geyser
out of them. His dictaphone flickers
as he carves his steak,
driving the knife from his elbows.

Afterwards, knees splayed on my
sofa, he gives my wife
a picture book of Libya.
Thick, menthol cocktails
obscure the bright glasses with green.

He and I trudge through the desert,
our waists roped together with shawls of sand.
I make my arrow; water salvoes
from his eyes. I feel a pulling
in the sand like a child who desires
nothing less than forever. At his nod,
the workers dig out
black oil.

He placed my wife in a spa that day
drinking tea with mint leaves, pungent
as frogs. When I find him oil,
I get my children back
from the soldiers' barracks
where he'd hidden them.
Their hair is lilacs,
lilacs.

Heretics

Churches fear heretics
more than those who never knew their secrets.

Heretics hurry home
with transubstantiated wine coppery in their mouths.
They spit it into a glass to do magic with.

Heretics slip
the communion wafer
into their top pockets
as the priest moves down the line.
They smoke it in a cigarette to impress their boyfriends.

Heretics know
the answers to the secret questions:
what happens after death,
how many hundreds of pounds
will ensure it doesn't happen to you.

I am finished with séances,
tables lumbering like alligators
after string-webbed fingers,
strangers' accurate insights
into my family problems.

I walk down the lane trailing the sacred Python
like a cotton draft excluder.

I know they are following me
in glossy BMWs. They will ensure it looks
like a chance hit and run.

(Imagined) Homecomings

Mick Dresses as a Zebra

My father is on his way home.
A sweaty zebra made of polyester
struggles to get his head on
over a mop of human hair
glossy as blackberries:
Mick had begged to be a dancing zebra
at our welcome-back carnival.
We lay out lemon sorbet, pastry cones
piped with white chocolate cream.

My father is on his way home,
his ship nearly reaches the terracotta shore
before vanishing with him in it.
We stand under ice-blue bunting
and cry at the empty sea.

I continue to spoon applesauce
into a bowl
that stays half-full.
The zebra-man tangles with himself:
when his shoulder is in the costume,
his knees pop out; when his knees are in,
a stray elbow jabs through the seams.

Strong Man and Vaudeville Girl

The bench tick-tocks.
A number '4' on my chest,
I size up my competitors.

A college girl in a peach tutu
with shiny straight hair
juggles many certificates,
posing briefly to display one at a time
whilst the others orbit her head.

A farm girl with milky skin,
roses pressed to her cheeks,
stronger than the strong man, throws
acrobats in green bodystockings
over her head. They somersault back to her
and end in a pyramid on her forearms,
breathing heavily.

The strutting queen of a provincial beauty pageant
loses her cool in this world-famous contest.
She sucks her pink throat-sweet into her lung
with a whimper. Her voice disappears
like water down a sinkhole
halfway through 'Hymn to Joy'.
When she insists on singing again,
her voice is tomato cans knocking
in a string bag.

I have painted my legs with coffee
to look like I'm wearing tights.
My pintacked shoes snap one-two
up to the strong man's cage.
The bars are hung with earrings and canapés.

My bow takes a minute; I flourish my arms.
The strong man grabs the two closest bars,
pulls them apart like a gum
driving a gap in two front teeth.
He collects himself, ready to step out of the cage.
I hold out my hands

        but the conjurer leaps in:
the beauty queen delayed us, it is time
for his trick. His white rabbits have not
been brought on, so
with a twist of his kid-gloved wrist
the conjurer makes the strong man vanish,

cage and all.

I Interview the President

I touch the bullet,
that last week almost scrunched my lung
to clingfilm,
three times inside my pocket
and dash from my crumbling hotel.

The president turns to greet me
in a house of gold mosaics:
tiled saints in brown rags proffer their eyes,
breasts, hearts on small dishes.

He offers me wine
in dragonfly-green glasses,
cake heavy with eggs, cracking
vertically with almond grains
that won't hug.

His sullen second daughter wears a galleon
cut from pearl on her lapel.
I imagine a man a century ago
poising a rock on a rope with one arched toe,
a net round his neck descending
through jellyfish romping
up and down in the waves,
no matter where they wanted to go.

I imagine the worm, the intruder
wriggling, breaking up cells in the oyster
then the nacre healing to a blister:
nothing's so smooth as pearl.

No fresh water
for the pearl fisher to wash in:
he would have had a salt exoskeleton for weeks,
each rub on his skin bubbling with white glister.

He yanks at the rope so his puller
on the boat can haul him to the air
so they can adorn
the president's daughter's navy-blue trouser suit.

The president's guards must have fled
as I was taping my interview.
Without a thought for me
he jumps spreadeagled over his other daughter,
pulls a pied marble table over them both.

A sniper-shot runs a crack down the wall,
hits a mosaic saint in the very act
of taking dictation with a goosefeather
from a pulsing red heart in the sky.

Under the saint's halved golden scalp
it is rough, clammy grey.

Satellite State

It's not like we could fly anyway;
after their shoals of sweets
glittering like the backs of beetles,
moving was hard.

I do not want to talk about the war,
our first introduction
to electricity,
but I will say they cut down all the trees:

no more poplars like lollipops,
birch trunks no longer
flaying wide-mouthed silver skins.
The visitors hold their guns up,

an angry forest arch
for us to dance under.
The leader accepts our kisses
as we emerge.

In the queue, I stretch
a length of piano wire.
beneath my coat. I will hold

        my hands up to him.

The Usual Ceremony

He saw what they did in other villages,
those figures in moleskin,
greasy black plumes
from birds continents away.

He has to let them
watch as he wobbles
on a raft in the centre of the lake,
his shoulders dancing
with their new diseases.

He bathed today
in a tin tank of vegetable oil.
His villagers unsacked
blizzards of gold powder
over him, rubbed the scanty rest
on themselves. Bronze beads
weight his eyebrows.

As usual, he hurls armfuls of treasure
into the water. Its surface shirrs
like a length of mink.

Five hundred years later,
the birch leaves' veins
are stodgy with glitter. Mice drink
spores of gold from the earth;
their guts pan
and pinch.

God

The whole research team
loops the loop
for miles inside a brilliant
metal cylinder. Our whoops
echo before we've opened our mouths.
Our bikes warp and lengthen.

What is the force that makes our brakes
wheeze and squeal,
the fringes of our lab-coats
tangle in spokes?

My father,
the reason for atoms,
a little confused. Dowel
under his clothing gives him
a splayed starfish shape.
He bounces
tissue-paper stars on strings.

Visitation

I was forbidden to tell
anyone that the twins were born
alive.

I began leaving bread and milk
in a saucer at night on the step
ever since the day I lay under the stream
balancing on my shoulder-blade tips,
counting.
Something pressed my forehead,
heavy as two sugar-sacks
until I crossed myself.

My feet stopped touching the ground
when I walked. I was given
plantain juice to weigh me down
each night in church.

When they began to trust me
to swallow it at home,
I dropped it in the sink,
floated

over the hills.

Winter Post

I was obsessed with hiding the flab
beating in my hatbox,
the smooth antlers surging slowly
against the oval cardboard lid.
I wasn't allowed to know
who scribbled the address on the side.

An upturned whale in the wood
tilts side to side,
lit orange with arm-linked silhouettes.
Cinnamon, sherry, nutmeg,
artichoke, plums, wine
served in its belly to the crack of clarinets.

Who is the fisher who turns to watch me?
The line twists in a malevolent
tongue, the lake chimes
with shaken ice. Is she
reeling it in or putting it back?
Let this be the last one.

I am nearly there when a bullet
wafts me downwards.
Snow mouths my shin,
elbow, forehead.

I drop my box,
the lid closes on me.

Early to Bed

The candidate for supreme ruler
is not trained for action
though he has a refined cologne:
basil oil and limeflower. Each photocall,
he makes sure to grasp something fresh, like an orange.
He remembers cloudberries, national in his hands.

When it comes, the disaster is quite trivial,
just a blast of ash coating his morning eggs
in black, tendrilled crusts. Their yolks stay ripe
as tacky paints. The roof sags, his aides
tell him never to go outside again.

He scrawls over the map of his country with charcoal;
in the margin, a cherub whips up hand-drawn waves
that crash like church organ
keys all jammed together.

The night is so long. The one-time candidate for supreme ruler
plans to learn the zither in his solitude.

Parsley Tea

I can't get enough of this
parsley tea. My mother is delighted.

She might suspect
my deadly purpose,
she might be happy
to know one of my desires,
as she melts and shrinks more heads
of parsley at the stove.

> *The frog prince's face*
> *is bland and secret*

The ginger roots' still-forming limbs
mummify with age.
For two days, seven hours, three minutes
I gag on parsley tea.
I am the witch that begged to exchange
a child for a herb.
I don't believe in folk tales.

> *Just as the website said,*
> *by the third day,*
> *I am bleeding.*

Mild herb, killing parsley,
the earth knows
her inhabitants love freedom.

> *he left*
> *before he arrived*

Maria

Reunion

I track his blood
through a quarter mile
of bars playing the Six Nations
in English. The earth tilts
us towards the sun.

Rooting in his shoulders,
salt arches triumphant feathers;
white armies stack
out of the briny puddle at his feet.

He has tanned like a houseplant
forgotten in a cupboard,
filling the shelves tamely
with frail exploring stems.

Waitresses proffer ham
pink and white as birth certificates,
shredded.

Ermines

My father keeps ermines in a sterile glass box,
strokes their coats' argent nightly
with his soft beige hands.
They wrap lovingly around his fingers.

Each day, he lays one ermine
on a purple runner on his kitchen table,
unscrews a bottle of muddy water
wrung from a dress found in the ocean
(the lipstick in the pocket
was perfectly useable,
though the wearer could no longer appreciate this).
With a pipette
he places an ounce of water
on the ermine's fur.

Invariably, the ermine stumbles
over its Tudor-style necklace
of lozenge-shaped gold links.
It cries a single tear
that tastes of a washed icing-bag,
rolls up like a tie for sale,
and dies.

Thus, my father tests the legend
that the ermine is so proud
of its unblemished white coat
it will die
rather than be dirty.

I decide to save the ermines,
gather them in a black cloth bag
from their box under his kitchen sink.
I choose to call them all, *Charles*.

They seem agitated;
I plan to knit them some toys,
try stroking them as my father does.

They die as soon as they feel my skin,
their mouths are frozen portcullises,
their glass-ball hearts
smashed as if between fingers,
the red plastic strings broken.

Cheetah

My father wasn't born a cheetah,
the shifts and buildups of sediments,
the growing and sinking of dark mountains
on sandy soil,
over eons
sped up to seconds
on his dappled, running skin.

But he did watch a huntsman on video
tracking a cheetah on foot for three days,
stroking it gently as it died.
The wise animal eyes
succumbed nobly to the sorrowing,
starving man .

Now a cheetah eyes my father, leashed
on a short rope, long-lashed,
pleading with sedatives
in a shack.
'I've cowed a child-killer,'
he tells himself, 'proud and stupid'.
He hands the baseball-capped guard
$500,
and shoots it in the head.

'Well done sir, great shot',
the keeper's hand is strong but my father
grips tighter. His sweat cools
as the keeper captures him
and the cold animal,
both steady and gaping
in a camera shot.

My father keeps the photo of himself
holding the cheetah like a swooning date
prominently on the mantel.

The 2.8 inch teeth,
the skull 7.5 inches in length.
He loves guests to assume
he shot well, even outran
this beast across the savannah.

At nights, I lie with her,
her deep-oiled fur soft on my bare feet.
Not encumbered with organs,
she seems to know so much.

The Cheapside Hoard

My father is splayed.
lap-lap, the pool in his villa.
doesn't care for his body.

Deft as a manicurist, I tweezer,
someone else's fingerprints
from icy gel
in the tall courier-box at my feet.

They quiver, white moths
on the third day of their three-day life,
and rest when I apply them
to my father's fingerpads.

I plug someone else's hair
into his scalp, dye it
to brassy corn.
Blood trickles over each sheaf:
lap-lap into the water.

My father erases
his love of rugby, his habit
of entering the few bars here
that show English TV.

I talk casually about the Cheapside Hoard.
The jewellery trade was secretive back then;
goldsmiths smashed cellar walls
to scurry undetected down whole streets,
with armfuls of amethyst grapes that crushed
would fill the mouth
with water. When promise-rings
cut with glass or dye managed
to hit the streets, those who made them
had their fingers cut off.

Elizabeth I had these bruisers,
I say, tugging the earring from his ear,
called 'voluntaries'. She let them earn so much money
dispensing rough justice of their own,
illegally, tidying the edges of society
without her getting her hands dirty.

I know they'll find the owner of the hoard,
I say, they can find the smallest split-hair nowadays.
My father waggles his new fingers.

He blanches only when I tell him
the owner of the Cheapside Hoard
died before he could enjoy his wealth.

Cutting Chips

A colander of potatoes on his head,
my father makes his light brown horse
curve its neck like an apple-slice,
using only a crooked baby finger
and spider-thin red thread
I could break with an eyelash.

I skin potatoes in the cellar,
Those soft bright hearts
that jump into my bucket
without an ounce of disloyalty,
my father kisses.
All tobacco-black rotten ones
he stamps to raw mash.

My own ventricles and chambers
seal up, drain of colour,
waiting for a safe spring
to tuber in.

CCTV cameras lean
like leopards all over my father's walls.
Some neighbours do get through the gate,
bringing pasteles, wine, business proposals.

Most remember my father stripping
all the clothes off the priest
and mocking him for two long hours.
Others recall conversations
about Montaigne and Spanish politics,
unsure where to put their
elbows on sofas propped
on elephant tusks.

Lobsters lumber gently across
the kitchen.
I kill them for my father
as he tears neon antennae,
leading straight to the government,
from his oldest potatoes.

Maria

Maria could not marry the man she loved
in church. So she placed two lead balls, pared
to the exact weight of her kneecaps
beside the altar. God thought
she was there, praying.

When she lifted her bouquet
in the registry office,
she was only thinking
of when the latch was too high
and she had been promised a stole
from the attic by her uncle.
After they'd seen the zoo, seen the caged rhino
swaggering round
a kind of wrecking-ball,
his only toy.

The clattering white teeth,
the numb whiskers, hooking her neck
quick as riptides. His wheedling,
'the what did you expect, when you asked for something
from the attic?' The door clicked shut.
The realisation all his movements
since the zoo were a straight line towards her
and the latch was too high,

but she was not there
she was in church, kneeling
white as the crocheted sea.

Maria Escapes the Party

The king of coins scowls
from the minor arcana.
Thunder rattles the glass
away from the window jamb
and Maria flows out

                    through the gap.

A leg points a toe, smokes
on the platter.
Our mouths regular as bootfalls,
our words the same jellied stock:
nice bouncy thigh,
where's Maria?

Maria's legs
lengthen and fur
as she kicks her heels
off at the sill.
Low, she eats

furmitory, marjoram, parsley;
seaweed, redcurrants, and clover.

X meets the CCTV Cameras

X has found her spitting image:
her nostrils have bedspring-
shapes, like young cucumbers.
She outlines her successor's nose in kohl
because spirits are first the smell of dank roses
pattied in children's fists.

X hands her successor her name:
The first letter is an ounce of seaglass,
the second a scrape of oleander
bobbling the wrist red.

Harebell-patterned curtains, thick and soft,
cover souls for whom death makes no difference.

The new X rubs herself with powdered iron.
It lifts like a cloak
as spirits once forgotten
surge through it, clench metal fists,
make scowls like those of people
robbing banks with tights over their heads.

The old X reverts to her real name,
Jenny.

Jenny hurries to the airport.
Her makeupless face turns, a sunflower
to the security cameras. At the scanners,
she keeps on one earring
(a steel hoop, a plastic pineapple)
so she will be patted down
comfortably
as someone screams behind the screens.
The guard winks at the little luxuries she tries to take through:
a box of bee-jelly, her right
sock bulging.

Fixed on their database,
which she imagines
to be thrillingly limitless, she is
waved on through
people with no papers.
She has passed.

The Laughing Gas Party

The limbless gleaming spirit
was salvaged from fir to help us. We
sucked, mouth to mouth, the canister.

One man's feet drum the floor
uncontrollably.

Anther takes an umbrella made
of stomach skin and flies
to the lemonade moon.

Maria sees a disembodied hand
paddling her collar bone. *I say*
say the men, *the best one yet*.

Maria is crying and crying, her cheeks
aching with mirth.

Dee

Bags of your clothes huddle in the cellar
like backs before an execution.

My name is written small in your diary
halfway down a list including Pat,
Lorelei, and Jaguar, and the note *I can't wait to meet*
all those guys who prefer pregnant women.

A sediment of posters
you made for your room:
DRINK WATER. DRINK WATER.
DON'T EAT DON'T EAT
scrawled on photos of your best friend,
words cupped in her full breasts,
over her innocent forehead.

The seeds I brought with me are firm as milk teeth,
light-filled, sweet.

His Difficulty with Jigsaws

His people
have steam train gratings for mouths,
sheet music trills in their foreheads,
sun rays and other people's faces
illuminate their pockets.

I right
him from where he's crashed.
big tears run down his nose, my nose:
He has lost
a piece of the sky.

Clepsydra

And God said, Let there be a firmament in the midst of the waters, and let it
divide the waters from the waters
                              —Genesis 1.6

I will measure out my life
in a home-brewing barrel.

I heft a full aquarium to the ceiling, tilt
it so water drips into the barrel beneath.

I glue lines of tiny shells on the barrel.
Each year, the water reaches a new line.

The crunch of typical clocks unbalances
me, like insects underfoot.

The waters on the ceiling
wrinkle round snails; they show their faces

slowly as stars. Leeches flow
downwards, priests in cassocks

hurtling
abysswards, shiver like oil-drops in the corners.

The edge of my garden
is a broken-backed stone beast, waiting. When the barrel is nearly full,

I jumble tarnished
silver apples in my jumper, mesh of rough cloth and glitter.

and, laughing, tears splashed to my cheeks,
bob for them

in all the years of my life.

Ops

My mum
fingers the plaster
where she patched me into the wall.

She sashays
between my father and the hollow
scraped in the brick where I hold
my breath,
when he comes home,
hungry,
wanting to pound her floral
wallpaper.

Afterwards, my father's
tummy
opens. A plush
red theatre curtain spills from the slit.

I tear through reams and reams
of this fabric.

        Where are
my brothers and sisters?